D1000267

To all who need hope —M. H.

FLAMINGO BOOKS

An imprint of Penguin Random House LLC, New York

First published in the United States of America by Flamingo Books,
an imprint of Penguin Random House LLC, 2023

Text copyright © 2023 by Michelle Houts
Illustrations copyright © 2023 by Sara Palacios

Penguin supports copyright. Copyright fuels creativity, encourages diverse voices, promotes free speech, and creates a vibrant culture. Thank you for buying an authorized edition of this book and for complying with copyright laws by not reproducing, scanning, or distributing any part of it in any form without permission. You are supporting writers and allowing Penguin to continue to publish books for every reader.

Flamingo Books & colophon are registered trademarks of Penguin Random House LLC.

Visit us online at penguinrandomhouse.com.

Library of Congress Cataloging-in-Publication Data is available.

Manufactured in China

ISBN 9780593206904

1 3 5 7 9 10 8 6 4 2

TOPL

Design by Monique Sterling
Text set in Horley Old Style

The publisher does not have any control over and does not assume any responsibility for author
or third-party websites or their content.

Hopefully the Scarecrow

Written by
Michelle Houts

Illustrated by
Sara Palacios

FLAMINGO BOOKS

A scarecrow stood in the garden.
Tall, proud, smiling.
Like most of us, he didn't remember
the very beginning of his days.

He only knew he was created
with loving hands.
Carefully crafted.
Wonderfully made.

He *did* remember the first time she placed him on his perch.

She set him up straight, stood back, and smiled.

"Hopefully, the scarecrow will keep the birds away," she'd said.

He hadn't known his name was Hopefully.

But he liked it.

Hopefully the Scarecrow also liked stories.
He couldn't read, of course,
        but she could.
Every day she brought her favorite books to the garden
        and she read to him.

And as she read,

the scarecrow journeyed over rocky cliffs,

and sailed rolling seas,

and met kings and queens and dragons

and other scarecrows.

He heard tales of courage and of hope.
And when she said, "The End,"
the scarecrow always felt a
little bit taller and braver.

One day, just after the beans withered,
and the cornstalks turned brown,
and the air became bitey and brisk,
her two sturdy hands lifted him from his perch
and placed him carefully in the shed.

"Hopefully, the scarecrow will be
okay in there all winter," she said.

He was alone, and the shed
was dark, but he was warm
and dry, and he didn't
worry because she had
said it herself:
he would be okay
during the long,
cold winter.
Besides, he had all her
stories nestled deep in the
straw beneath his hat to keep
him company.

Finally, when the scarecrow heard the birds return from
the south, and daylight lingered past dinnertime,
and the air smelled fresh and green,
the thin crack of door light widened,
and he was once again returned to the garden.

Year after year, she came
and she read to him.

As the books got bigger,
the stories got scarier,
and funnier,
and sweeter.

And year after year, just after the beans withered,
and the cornstalks turned brown,
and the air became crisp and brisk,
her two sturdy hands would lift him from his perch and
place him carefully in the shed.

"Hopefully, I'll see you in the spring!" he heard her say
one fall just before she closed the door.

That next spring,
    after the scarecrow heard the birds return
    from the south,

and daylight lingered past dinnertime,
        and the air smelled fresh and green,
    the thin crack of door light widened,
and two different hands placed him in the garden, where he,
Hopefully, waited.
After all, she had said she'd see him in the spring.

But she didn't come to read to him.

The next day, a soaking rain made the
scarecrow's flannel droop,
   and thunder shook the ground
   beneath his wobbly legs.
   But he was not discouraged.

Day after day, the summer
sun glared, and soon
the scarecrow's smile
started to fade.

Once, a mean wind shoved him
sideways and took his hat
far away.

Still, she did not come.
And the scarecrow
was lonely.

Her stories filled his head,

and he remembered that to journey over rocky cliffs,

and sail rolling seas,

and face monsters,

one must be brave.

So he, Hopefully, waited,

for a very long time,

until . . .

. . . one day, two familiar hands straightened his perch and smoothed his weathered shirt.

"Oh my, look at you!" she said. "Hopefully, I can fix this!"
With some patches, a dab of paint, and a new straw hat,
the scarecrow's smile brightened.

He wondered if she'd brought new stories,
  but her hands were empty.
    And when she lifted him, perch and all, from the
      garden, the scarecrow was confused
        but not afraid.
They were going somewhere.
Together.

"Hopefully the Scarecrow will love it here," he heard her say.

And he knew she was right.